To Lilli – our own faerie and earth child!
All our love to you this Christmas.

Aunt Karen, Uncle Al,
Collin and Brendon

CHILD OF FAERIE

CHILD OF EARTH

Written by **JANE YOLEN**   Illustrated by **JANE DYER**

LITTLE, BROWN AND COMPANY

Boston   New York   Toronto   London

Special thanks to Andrei and Rachael

Text copyright © 1997 by Jane Yolen
Illustrations copyright © 1997 by Jane Dyer

First Edition

Library of Congress Cataloging-in-Publication Data

Yolen, Jane.
    Child of faerie, child of earth / written by Jane Yolen ; illustrated by
Jane Dyer.— 1st ed.
        p.   cm.
    Summary: One Halloween night, a fairy child befriends a human
child and together, they explore each other's worlds but neither wants
to give up his or her own home.
    ISBN 0-316-96897-8
    [1. Fairies—Fiction.   2. Friendship—Fiction.   3. Halloween—
Fiction.   4. Stories in rhyme.]   I. Dyer, Jane, ill.   II. Title.
PZ8.3.Y76Ch   1997
[E]—dc20   95-35501

10   9   8   7   6   5   4   3

NIL

Published simultaneously in Canada by Little, Brown & Company
(Canada) Limited

Printed in Italy

To Adam and Betsy,
wayfarers in faerie — J. Y.

To Vivien,
who carries the light
—J. D.

He was a child of faerie folk,

A child of sky and air,

And she was a child of humankind,

Of earth and toil and care.

      They met in the dusk of Hallow's Eve,

      When widows grieve

      In widow's weave.

      They met in the dark of Hallow's Eve,

She had flowers in her hair.

"And where do you go, O child of earth?
Oh, why do you wander here?
Are you not afraid of the faerie race
Whose castles are so near?"

　　"My mama says there's no such thing
　　As faerie wing
　　And elven ring.
　　She says there's never been such thing,
And I should have no fear."

He took her by her dirt-soiled hand
And led her to his hall.
He showed her brownies and boggles and sprites
And elven folk and all.

    She ate the grass, she drank the dew,

    The faerie brew

    Of rainbow hue.

    She danced all night with the elven crew

And didn't sleep at all.

"Oh, stay with me, dear human child,
Become a child of night.
We'll dance between the hollow hills
Bedecked in candlelight.

And ever after, Hallowe'en,
Clothed all in green,
My faerie queen,
You'll be the loveliest ever seen,
The elven court's delight."

She looked around the faerie hall
Beneath the hollow hill,
And all the glamour round her spun
To bend her to his will.
    But with a sigh, she shook her head.
    "That's not my bread
    And drink," she said.
    "I cannot on your food be fed
And still my needs fulfill."

"But since I've danced with you this night,
This day you dance with me."
She took him by his grass-green sleeve
And led him over the lea.

     She led him down the farmyard road,
     Past meadows mowed
     And gardens hoed.
     She led him over the human road,
And full of awe was he.

They stroked the cat, they milked the cow,

They fed each chick and hen.

He marveled at the sounds and smells

Of barn and yard and pen.

He drank cold milk and ate brown bread.

He made a bed.

He cleaned a shed.

He followed everywhere she led,

Then round about again.

"Oh, stay with me, dear faerie child,
And live here on the land.
We'll till the soil, we'll plow the field,
We'll harvest hand in hand.
    The night is fair, but day is best,
    So be my guest,
    Forget the rest."
    And on and on her suit she pressed
With strong and sure demand.

He looked around the human world,
A world of gold and brown,
A world where farmyard turns to village,
Village into town;

A world of colors pure and bright,
Of open sight,
Of warm sunlight,
Unlike the shadowed world of night,
Of moon and thistledown.

He thought about the faerie halls,
The faerie queens and kings.
He thought about the cold, cold stars
That shone on faerie rings.

"I miss my own; I cannot stay.

You work. I play.

I must away.

I'll keep the night and you the day."
He stretched translucent wings.

"Oh, wait, oh, wait," she cried to him.

"At least a gift I'll give,

Reminding you that here above

Is where a friend does live."

And through the daylight world again,

Past denizen

Of barn and pen

She tracked past horse and cow and hen

To find a gift to give.

At last she found a fresh hen's egg,

A gift from humankind

So he'd remember earth and toil

When he'd left both behind.

    Then in return, he touched the shell,

    And with a spell

    Of fare-thee-well

    Extracted from that fragile shell

A feather to remind.

"I give you this that comes from that,"
The faerie child replied,
"That egg and feather both shall serve
As token and as guide.

    That we may both go arm in arm
    And fear no harm,
    Nor take alarm
    When visiting in hall or farm
(Or other lands beside)."

The gifts exchanged, they each went back
To homes they loved full well.
But now and then, they visited,
Helped by a faerie spell.
    And though the years flew quickly past,
    They were friends fast,
    From first to last,
    Which left all skeptics flabbergast
At how they did so well.

So if one lucky Hallow's Eve,

You hear the night birds sing

And see a child of faerie guise

With bright and gauzy wing

 A-flutter in a moonlit glade

 And all arrayed

 In silver shade,

 Be bold, be brave, be unafraid,

And join that faerie ring.